# If I Don't Find Pleasure I Will Die

## *poems by*

## Roger W. Langton

SCARECROW BOOKS

## ACKNOWLEDGMENTS

Thanks is given to the following magazines where some of the poems in this book first appeared: *Wine Rings, Second Coming Magazine, Nitty-Gritty, In A Nutshell* and *The Westerly Review.*

Cover photo by the Author
Photo of the Author by Paul F. Fericano

ISBN: 0-916296-04-0

**SCARECROW BOOKS**
1050 Magnolia, #2
Millbrae, CA 94030

*for Ann Menebroker*

Roger W. Langton

# FOREWORD

It is certainly not difficult for me to offer genuine praise for Roger Langton's poetry. What is immediately experienced in this man's poetry is that you can get damn close to him through his words and feel the heat, but never get burned out. This, I feel, can be easily explained due to the fact that as a poet, Langton immediately recognizes the all important need *not* to remain the same, but to experiment with his work and know that change is essential, however gradual, to the survival of his art.

Mediocre poets will receive a handful of praise and then end up living in a dark cloud with a condescending frown, distorting anything that is real. These poets dress up like the *dead* and fool no one but themselves. On the other hand, good poets are the ones who undoubtedly live with the knowledge that sometimes the "ego" does tend to blur the real work that must be done in order to further their poetry—its growth, its life. They accept this, but learn to put it aside and get down to work.

Roger Langton undoubtedly falls into this latter group and is destined to go even farther—not because he is a good poet only, but because he is finding the right direction that will inevitably keep him *alive* long after the words have been written, read and appreciated.

—*Paul F. Fericano*
Millbrae, California
April 20, 1977

## A FOOTPRINT

i cleared the house
of all reminders.

(being stung every day
had to stop.)

i threw away three
ghosts hanging in
the closet.

hid the books,
stopped playing the records,

buried the photographs in
lost places.

much later,
while working in the garden,
i uncovered

a footprint—

baked—
solid as the reality of our
past.

# ANOTHER ONE OF THOSE DAYS

the clock strikes thirteen
while an ant runs for cover
only to be crushed by
a wind-blown garbage can
a bird sings a rusty song
that falls apart
in mid flight and
scatters the rock-concert
potters who rush to their
japanese cars and
squash for cover within
the remade beer cans that
once shared the beach with
volleyballs and lovers
each hour sends a
message of hope
that rips the black off
of italian women and tickles
the tails of young girls
who see clearly the need
for breakfast at the
dawn of each day
a bee zooms by and
lands on a car bumper
stinging the chrome
staining it yellow
until washed by
the great unwashed who
see the circus and
laugh without understanding
what is happening

# AFTER A DAY TEACHING ANTHROPOLOGY

i remember
the earlier voice;
i knew then;
now — nothing,
like aristotle.
i see clearly
corners, angles—
no longer obstacles.

originality — creativity,
deceptions taught by
false prophets.
students being prepared
for a life that
doesn't exist.

my own place,
an alien culture,
quaint as savages with
strange ways.
ideas, wrapped in people,
paper, invite me in
but i cannot enter
anymore.

## LAST VISIT WITH GRANDFATHER

i almost didn't see him
that last time
but i forced it.
i called up and said that
i knew he was disappointed
about me marrying young;
(shortly after our long talk
about not marrying young)
he told me to come over
that he admired the prose
of my letter breaking
the news.

i arrived early
shook his weakened hand
then startled him with
childhood's wet kiss.

he told me of his life
why grandmother died early
that he was still potent
at age seventy-two.
in his basement hide-away
we viewed his films of
indian country.
it was a good time that stays
with me these fifteen years.

next morning
over bacon and eggs
he told me familiar stories
advisory tales
encouraged me to accumulate
be rich.

when we parted
i saw more clearly who i was
that i would reflect grandfather
it was unique to be able to
say a final good-bye
for him to know that
i would carry on.

two months later the phone call came:
grandfather was dead
died while showing his movies
just a few weeks before the birth of
his great-grandson, my son,
who would carry the name.

# INCEST

i recall the day
i explained the
oedipus complex
to my mother
right after
i had my first
lecture on freud

she never trusted me
after that
and told strange
stories
to the mothers
of potential
wives

i still can't love
her name
or the names
of my sisters

# RESISTING HANDS

the wind is spinning
circles
of string
making knots in
treeless landscapes
swirling
in and out of
synagogues before
prayers are finished
swearing promises
on faultlines
shattering to pieces
of pain
liberation
building life-lines
of hot plastic

scarring
resisting hands

# THE RUNNING GRAVE

"When, like a running grave, time tracks you down . . ."
                                                    —*Dylan Thomas*

i glanced quickly to
my side and
saw the running grave
keeping pace with every
step
i burst forth with
all my strength
but i could not leave
death behind
or cause it to outrun
my shadow

i tried all the tricks
i knew
hid in a camouflaged bush
dove deep into the water
took a jet to london and
timbuktu
but the grave
the running grave
kept pace with every
subtle move

## HOW TO MAKE A MIRROR
## INTO A WINDOW

one day
i'll scrape
the black
off the back
of my mind,
vacuum up
the trash,
haul it to
the dump and
see clearly
the view of
myself.

## SECOND COMING

every once in awhile
i hear bits of talk about
this guy named jesus who
is supposed to show up and
make some big changes
i hear that he came once before
that he was discovered by
three wise men
only to be nailed by a king
who thought that he
was trying to take over
he said that he would come back
millions of people light candles
and wait
after two-thousand years i
wonder why they don't give up
but they say it is all beyond
human understanding anyway
i am told that when he gets
here he will make everybody
be good and will punish the
wicked by some objective
set of celestial norms set
down by sociologist advisors
but then he is supposed to be
a superstar who will put on
the perfect rock concert
where mankind will pop pills
in the world-wide lockstep
of instant clarity
the trouble is that i like
the world the way it is and
if this guy does come i'll
put hard questions to him

if he doesn't have good answers
i'll have to go out and
find an alternative candidate
i keep doing what i do but there
is something nagging about this
story and on occasion after
a couple of beers i look up
into the night sky and see if
any new stars have appeared

## SPORTS

balls—
all sizes
going in and out of things
up and down
bouncing
flying
rolling.

crowds—
voices pumping
tribal chants
frenzy
loyalty.

uniforms
for the seduction of
las vegas
pom pon girls.

the extra young
diverting
sexuality
until ready
for the real thing
and
the extra old
trying to hide
from death.

## BOSWELL

boswell, the cat, died
a few days back.
he never considered death
or had a notion to inquire
philosophically—
he just died.
perhaps he never knew
he lived.
a full dish
and a she-cat were all
that held him to life.
i hardly held him
or took much notice,
except to see that i didn't
slam him in the door.

i bought the copper-eyed
white fur ball from janet
(not knowing then that she
would be my lover).
boz was a leo, like me,
born on the same day too.

i dug a hole in the backyard
and he's there now—
only five-years old.

i feel guilty, of course, for
those times of neglect,
but i'll get over it.

## ODE TO THE GIRL IN THE
## FIFTIES WHO SAID YES

no silly-talking boy
becomes a man
until he has loved
a woman

in the fifties
restless boys sought
manhood in fantasy
secret night stroking

real girls said NO

(no wonder such fuss
was made over a showing
slip or a peek-open blouse)

thanks goes to the
girl in every school
who would meet boys in
the park

she had a bad reputation
called all sorts of names
slut
loose woman
and worse

nobody married her
nobody knows her now
yet
nobody forgets her
boys become men are
grateful for

the MARTYR      the SAINT

## THE BLUE CHAIR

the blue chair
fits like a shoe
expands
contracts
as i grow fat
thin
to satisfy lovers

inward life passes
here
reading        writing
making poems
thinking
of faded flowers
planting
imaginary seeds

i search
under the cushion
and find treasures
from the past

# WHITE HOOD FADES TO YELLOW

the hill-belly man sat on
the cracker barrel,
fat flowing over the sides
like wax down a candle stick—
a divine-right king yelping
at the beards who climbed
the creaking steps.

he was white superior,
from the best klan stock
found in those parts.
he knew,
absolutely,
the right from the wrong—
no nagging birds flying to
disturb his peace.

"if you don't like it,
you can leave the country"
was a favorite expression,
along with: "those northern
nigger-lovers, what they doing
around here anyhow"?
a real seeker after truth.

he worked hard at the
judgement occupation,
spoke his mind clearly while
waiting in the welfare line—
hated bums, "too lazy to
work", he said, "too much
trash around these parts".

and the wood whittling went
on for weeks turned to years.
now he speaks with mumbled
breath as his
white hood fades to yellow.

the black customers pay no
heed to the old man who
sits in front of the store.

## ABSTRACT POEM

nothing sings like the
saw that tears flesh
and makes a shine
upon the victim's
shoe.
it's a buzzsaw shine that
attracts bees
that skip and skate
off windowpanes;
out,
let me out to the
real peach blossoms
away from the plastic
sitting in
the living room!

nothing sings like the
whip
with a breakfast cereal
crackle that licks
the flesh of infants,
grabs the bottle and
smashes it white on
the floor of middle income
habitations.

how often does jazz
make a play of sense that
is nonsense and
push the mind into the
open furnace until
it ashes and blows away
by swirling skirts?

## LOYALTY

when her breath
made glass-ring
vapor on my neck
and my heart
started pumping
messages
of sensitivity,
i knew
that it was time
to cork the bottle,
return it to the
cellar,
deep down in
the coolest
corner—

after all,
her husband was
my best friend.

# A VISIT MADE, ANOTHER POSTPONED

confessions come hard for hank
but he had to let it out

he told me of a visit to
a cat house when he was
a married man
he needed a woman
his wife was away and he
thought that it wouldn't
mean anything

he said that his god grabbed
him right in the middle
of the embrace and all he
could think of was that
a whore was a whore
who smelled of the sperm
of the thousand who
came before

he walked away feeling dirty
discontent
unable to attend mass
for months
never to confess to
the dracula who hides behind
the curtain and
fears the light of the cross
as much as any sinner

## DON'T GO AWAY FOREVER

you are the ax
that cuts the stem
of your own bloom.
the wilting
puts age upon my face.

yet,
stroke my open hand;
it will never
make a fist.

let friendship be
the healer.

## EMILY

i think of her
hiding in dark
victorian rooms,
living again an
aborted romance,
peeking from
the staircase.

i write of
life,
pain,
love.
she made riddles,
clever puzzles,
games.

i have less time.
but she *was* time
in sweaty clothes,
passion consumed
in words.

she,
a better poet.
me,
a finer gift.

## FOR ANNIE

we write
back and forth
with light's speed
each message
a release of
what is never spoken
a promise
that agitates
never settles
a warm
sweet bath of
intimacy that
never cools and
spawns bubbles
throughout
the day

# NOT UNTIL AFTER CHRISTMAS

it happened that sunday
in december when everybody
was talking of war,
the end of all of us.
i was confused about this
sudden disruption of
frog searching and cowboy
games.

i had never seen so many
adults upset,
all at the same time and
with such worried looks of
somber intensity.
i wandered through the
neighborhood
a lost boy
crying.

a group of my friends got
together for comfort.
we stood in the middle of
the street, full of questions
and silence.
we were all scared until one
kid said not to worry because
the japs wouldn't come until
after christmas.

## PROVING THAT I EXIST
## CAN BE FATAL

i kick stones and
hear the billiard-ball
sound of
cracking heads

encouraged by
this proof that i exist
i move on to
boulders and
buildings
until my
imprint
is felt
like the noose seizing
the neck at that
final instant

## SAUNDRA'S LETTER

i was playing pool when
her letter came
it was handed to me by a
fellow captive who was
innocent of its impact

return address    saundra    arizona

her name shut out    the pool
the place    the people    the world
i didn't expect to
hear from her again

i recalled our last evening together
we went to a dance
had a fine time
she told me that she loved me more
than ever

later we parked in my
poor man's car and i felt
her sweater-tight breasts and
made my way up her
petticoat-filled skirt
(red and white    i remember red and white)

she became offended and
despite her rapid breath and expansive
gyrations
she called me a sinner
said she did not want to see me again and
sent back the necklace

her grandmother talked to the bishop
i was called in and
told to repent

i was idiot enough to give my consent
to put my passion in a drawer until
i could let it out under
the sacred covers of a marriage bed
rage   rage   rage
i should have gone directly to a whore

i began to look for salvation elsewhere

a few weeks later i was off to heidelberg
not to be a student prince but
a uniformed blight that stalked
the streets near the haupstrasse

i had been away for a year when
that letter came

i learned that dicky was dead
that her grandmother was fine
and that maybe just enough feeling was left
to be worth a letter

i did see her again
even asked her to marry me      she said no
which turned out to be a good reply because
i saw her four children later and discovered
that i would have been bored
beyond suicide and that my current wife
was much better because she didn't
think of me as a sinner at all

## BEGGING BOWL EYES

we walked to the creek,
felt the cold water.
rocks put dents in
our feet.

i recaptured
my childhood creek.
she was making her
memories.

tiny spring fishes
swarmed
making a hawk's shadow.
she scraped up a few,
carried them home in
an old tin can.

(it was one of those
times when she was called
my daughter. we ran,
shared intimate laughter.)

the photos remind me.

one small fish remains.
i am moved to meet its
begging bowl eyes.

## ANY HAND

hand reaches
 crib encloses
  innocence in search
 to life a pen
  callous in a field
   pain    joy
all the same
 chance
  time teaches
sorts    classifies
 palm withers
  the hand reaches

# HAVE WE COME SO FAR?

how long does it take and
have we come so far?
we till separate plots that
plant beyond our lives.

the pilgrim swamp—
compact folk.
the midwest dirt plower who
made us all rich.
the wheel makers who spread
us about—
the best place,
always the best place.

how long does it take?
judges swivel in their chairs,
whisper dirty stories that
become bolder and balder.
law unfolds like a decaying
scroll.  have we come so far?

is there a lion that wants to
lie with a lamb or an ant that
steps aside for a fellow worker?
how long does it take and
have we come so far?

# ALWAYS DOESN'T LAST VERY LONG

karen said she would
love me always
(i have letters to prove it)
after our divorce
janet
christine and
kerstin
(in that order)
told me they would love me
always

for christine and
kerstin
i was their first always
and they couldn't understand
why i laughed when
they said it
but they will think of me now
and laugh too

too bad really
maybe i shouldn't have
laughed at all

## DARK OF LIFE

i see her daily
and i am quick to
sense that closest
hope of sexuality
a young girl
recently arrived
and innocent of
lust

a shyness keeps me
in this room
dark of life
yet full of semen that
lacks the courage
to be buried in
the belly of
a whore
or venture forth
to take her
last day of childhood

# THE OLD MAID'S TABLE

i laughed
at the old maid's table,
salad bowl of stars
and crusty old men,
meat fried stiff
with rusty sides
and rows of running
diamonds.
the crystal glasses
with microscopic spots
sang tunes of remorse,
sipped to lips parted
by a thousand
conversations.

a tiny fork
worn smooth from
prestigious polishing
sat warmly near my hand
inviting me
to stun the juices
of a maiden's
secret places.

my laugh turned to
painless tears.
the tender gesture left
peace at the end of
an old maid's day.

## WOMAN IN BLACK

in every church
sits a woman dressed
in black
a raven
that pecks holes in
wooden benches
lights candles for
the dead

she stands
on every street corner
a cinder that stoops
over a flower stand
waits to turn to
ash

each day she visits
the coffin of her man
places her body inside
and beckons little girls
to follow

## WHERE?

memories
seldom come anymore:
the day we went fishing,
stood on the white rock,
laughed;
a sing in the car when
i admired your voice;
you,
dead drunk on the couch—
(i cried hard in an
empty room);
the fight—
(i raped your fatherhood);
your gentleness
born of a sainted mother;
anger that sapped you
to an empty shell.

i want to find more
good feelings,
record them instead;
but where?
surely there is more
somewhere—
surely.

## WALKING IT OFF

feeling close in like
a room without windows
i walk outside
count oil stains on
the sidewalk and
whisper thoughts like
the old men who
talk to the concrete of
big cities

it's a crazy time when
all is discontent and
i don't care if i ever
return to familiar places
i say all i would say as
if the if were walking by
my side

finally
i empty out
end the turmoil that brought
me through unfamiliar streets
after a short rest on a curb
i stand up and head back home

## TEST DAY

the students sit
at their desks
tap out morse code essays
directed by the teacher's key.

they frown,
intense from parental hopes
and opaque delusions—
conditioned by a thousand episodes
no longer remembered.

the other selves emerge
as red faces or rapid turns
of the head.
light falls from fluorescent gods
that disavow the shadows.

a boy in the corner
wads up his paper,
smiles
and, without permission, walks out
of the room.

he will have to report to the dean
and be asked again
to give up his sanity.

## TOOTHLESS JUAN

he wasn't much to
look at and i had to
defend him at least
three times a week
from the sneers of
snobbish companions
but i called him friend
we met in an old bar
near mazatlan
the floor was dirt
and everyone toothless and
old but juan had a
warmth that opened me
we drank together and
swapped irrational stories
in distorted spanish
he made fun of the
government and joked
about pancho villa and his
revolutionary women
i spoke of old nixon and
the military-industrial
complex
we passed many hours that
way before i went back to
the turista part of town
i saw him every summer for
several years until that
last visit when i couldn't
find him anywhere
nobody could tell me where
or who he was exactly
just poor old toothless juan
who was famous because he
knew a gringo from california

## THE GREAT CATHEDRAL

there are times when
all of us walk boldly
into the great cathedral
when we put aside thoughts
of papal corruption
idols and
the zealots who burn books
and judge     judge
judge     ad     infinitum
we go because there is
no place else to go
all props are gone
the play has ended and
we need the illusion
of tomorrow
a reason to survive the day

## IS THIS A POEM?

sitting in bed,
my head propped by
two pillows,
i read karl shapiro
and think that i can
write as well,
wonder why he is great.

am i not covered with
books?
am i not filled with driven
words?
am i not shuffled by card
players—
likely to get the final
ace?

it could be the soft bed
or walls that stop me.
i'll put my bed outside,
see what comes from nosy
neighbors—weather or not.

but is this a poem?
what other form could describe
it?
what happened to annabell-lee,
the sea,
foot, meter and rhyme to disci-
pline me?

## GOING BACK

going back doesn't make
the hope but we have to
test because it seems
warm like a child's
pajamas—everything
smaller, older than decay
but the grown-up world
is full of pitfalls, worse
than when we first learn
about hot, the street and
the boogie man in the
closet. we hold tight to
the teddybear and our
fingers wear out blanket
edges. mommies and daddies
become mothers and fathers
but we can't help going back
to take one hard look and
then never look again.

## VICTIMS

sitting in a restaurant
i think of the
displaced-aggression dog
and the wall that
gets a kick because
the man lost his money in
a crap game.

i consider the innocents
who become the target of
dart games—who get stuck
because somebody
sees circles on them with
a bulls-eye middle or
the waitress who doesn't
get a tip because the people
at the next table can't
keep their brats quiet.

angry,
i get up and walk out before
the food arrives.

## LOSS OF FAITH

i don't recall the exact
moment he died;
perhaps it was in that one
sociology class too many
or while camping at big sur
when i felt a sudden cold.

for ten years i knew him
as a prop to claim love,
to pray and to satisfy
ego needs.
when he died there was no
special funeral,
just a feeling of being free,
yet all alone—
absolutely alone.

others,
long before nietzsche have
faced a good-bye to hope.
for me it was no shock,
only a disappointment.

i continue to wear bright
colors and to dance but now
there is no stage for future
performances.

i steal a glance into the coffin
every now and then to make sure
it remains empty;
it always is,
but maybe one day.

## PROJECTION

why does the
self-stroking ax
chop you to tiny pieces,
each fragment a
distorted representation
of self?

every love poem rips.

warm words ricochet,
unheard.

the confetti of
new year's eve has more
purpose.

## PIZZA PARLOR ROMANCE

it was a blind date

we were supposed to go
to a movie but the baby
sitter didn't show
she brought her five-year
old who wouldn't let us
get to know each other

at thirty-four she was
great to look at but
she would fade fast now
and become a cranky
all-american-beauty-rose
reject

she got up several times
and wiggled her way to
the ladies' room like a
fisherman's silver lure
i was supposed to bite but
i pretended not to notice
like the legendary trout
people come miles to try
and snare

i sat across from her
saw that i could have her
then be discarded like her
other pizza parlor dates

i tried hard but
ended up being nobody but
myself
i shook my head
walked away and decided that
i'd rather be alone

## BEING SINGLE IN A WORLD WHERE THE ONLY PLACE TO GO IS NOAH'S ARK

the call went forth to gather
two by two
i don't know who sounded the
call but everybody
except the wee babes responded
neighbors were paired
friends were paired
adolescents
bears
circus clowns
pigs
spiders and
geese
were all paired
a sexual celebration
even the pears were paired

there were a few exceptions
a graduate student or two
covered with dust in some
academic library or
the mad people locked away
in the silly factories
but i didn't see them and
didn't know
(poor man
i guess he will always be a loner)

i asked noah what i had to
do to get a ride on his ship of pairs
he said go hither and thither
and find a woman
bring her to me
as your wife
and i will make a place for
you

I took right off
i didn't want to be left out
i ran all over the world
trying to come up with
somebody
anybody who would be my ticket

i even asked a persian whore
with moth-ball breasts
invisible teeth and
a greedy family that shouted
do   do   say yes
to the empty glass
we require a very small bride price
for poorer class of tourist
she finally said no
said she got sea sick too easily
(maybe he should meet aunt sam
she will make somebody a wonderful wife)

another woman showed some interest
but her husband wouldn't give permission

when i got back
exhausted
i stood alone
noah said   sorry
breeding pairs only
(no partner   no bridge)

i pleaded
said that i couldn't swim
that i could be the resident
ark poet that would sing praises
shout hosannas to land crabs and
maybe be useful as a cabin boy
or clean up
all that animal   paired shit

but he remained firm
he was sure of his orders

47

i tried to sneak aboard
but was spotted by a mouse
that told a rat
that ran to noah and
i was hauled off by
two bengal tigers
i tried again
this time dressed as a banana
but some damn gorilla peeled me
and i almost got my head
bit off

i hung around for several days
there was no place to go
then
all    of    a    sudden
it started to rain like
a lindberg ticker-tape parade
i ran for shelter
climbed and climbed
stood on the highest mountain
where i watched the ark
float away

i was quiet for awhile

then
i raised my fist into the air
shouted my determination
to learn to tread water
and one day find noah and
tell him
where to get

## THE DOOR IS AJAR

the door is ajar
jammed by god's hand
like a salesman's foot.
the house mouse looks out
and the woodworm struggles
to make its way.

the door is ajar
held stir by the angry
wand of santa claus.
the cats peek, sneak and
jelly beans await their
turn to try.

the door is ajar
managed by the ghosts of
frightened servants who listen
to the whispers of
masters.
the see-saw wanders through
the crack and whines.

the door is ajar
opened by the charm of the
ugly clown who beckons the
shadows to enter.
the oiled eye looks through
the keyhole and
keeps the hinges in
quiet tune.

to close the door behind
would be far too simple—
far too,
      too far,
          far too.

## IF I DON'T FIND PLEASURE
## I WILL DIE

the tip sticks out
like the unintended
consequence of
human starvation—
just enough to
offend the clergy
but not enough to
stir the common
man.

i rub my
finger over it,
feel the prick of
unsatiated morality,
cover the window to
avoid the reflection
of my intent and
enter gently into
pleasure.